JULIE ABNETT

SNOOKUMS AND SQUIDDLE

SAVE
FLUFFY
THE
RABBIT

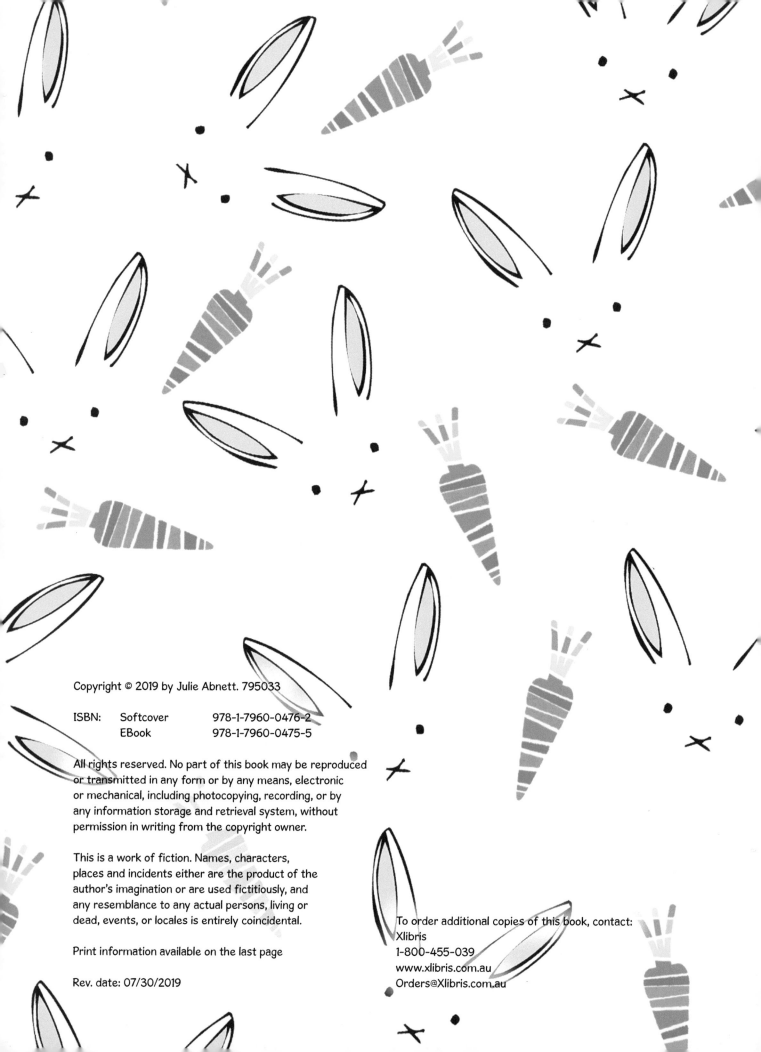

Print information available on the last page

Rev. date: 07/30/2019

To order additional copies of this book, contact:
Xlibris
1-800-455-039
www.xlibris.com.au
Orders@Xlibris.com.au

Tom and Molly lived in the country. One morning, Molly discovered Fluffy her pet rabbit was missing.

Molly and her big brother Tom, also their two pet dogs, Snookums and Squiddle would go on their first, of many exciting, adventures.

Throughout the day, but especially on their way home, Tom and Molly talked about all the wonderful animals plus all the other magical things they seen, plus things that had happened.

Molly thought to herself as they were nearly home, that she knew she would dream about their adventure especially the parts that was like a fairy tale.

Tom and Molly talked about how grateful they were to live in the country, as they opened the large gate that lead them up past the lovely roses, their subtle perfume this time, was overpowered by their mother's cooking., As Tom said to Molly, "it's good to be home.'

CHAPTER ONE

Tom and Molly lived in a quaint cottage, deep down in beautiful valley that was surrounded with acres of lushes greenery, wild yellow daisy's mixed with patches of Patterson course here and there as far as the eyes could see, and if one was luckily enough to get closer to the foot hills, that is another delightful place. But most of all if you look down into and around the valley from the very top, what a glorious site of all sites, was the river, which ran so gracefully behind all four country cottages which were situated distantly down and around in the valley.

One day as Tom and Molly were playing with Squiddle and Snookum's their favorite pet dogs, Molly happened to glance over and noticed that fluffy her little white rabbit was gone.

Tom and Molly raced over with Snookum's and Squiddle only to find that a fox had dug under Fluffy's house and let him out. Molly cried and cried as she managed to say, "I hope nothing has happened to Fluffy." Molly felt so upset, she looked at Tom with heart break in her eyes.

She said, "Tom will you help me look for him please?'

"Yes, he said eagerly.'

Molly began to slowly calm herself; she began looking everywhere. She quickly searched under the bushes near their cottage. Meanwhile Tom scrambled in amongst all the tall blue lavender that lined the side of their quant country cottage.

"Have you found fluffy yet,' Tom asked anxiously?

"No,' Molly replied quite concerned'

"Well, please don't be upset.' Tom replied as he stood up and dusted himself down.

"Molly don't worry, we will find him.'

"Yes,' she answered looking up at him.

"Perhaps, Fluffy has run off somewhere way out in the field to get away from that fox.'

"Do you really think so, Tom?'

"Well Molly, you would run away and hide too if a fox came after you.'

"oh yes I would,' said Molly. Now I am frightened for Fluffy.'

"Please Tom, can we go and look for Fluffy.'

"Yes Molly, but I will go and ask mother first to make sure that it's alright.

CHAPTER TWO

After a few moments Tom came back outside and said, "Mother said it was alright to go as long as we don't wonder too far away, 'she also made us a couple of drinks to take with us.'

The children started walking towards the big gate, they passed their mother's beautiful garden, which was filled with large marigolds at the back then all sorts of different colored petunias. Red and white roses followed both sides of the drive way that lead out into the open fields. Snookums decided that they wanted to go too. They barked, pouncing around and around Tom and Molly so excitedly until Theodore the big back cat plunged out in front of them and raced off.

Now Squiddle and Snookums knew that Theodore was forever trying to torment them. So away they went, Snookums then Squiddle ran as fast as they could nearly knocking Molly and Tom over. They raced across the grass past the pond, darting through the chickens until they came to the pig sty where Theodore, had perched himself up on a tall wooden post just tormenting Snookums and Squiddle.

The children called out to the dogs, after a while, they came running. When the dogs caught up to Tom and Molly they all continued through the field until they came to a cow track, that guided them to a small dam.

Squiddle and Snookum's seen two ducklings, they raced over to them and began to bark. The drake was on the bank with the mother duck flapping their wings vigorously, pretending that they couldn't fly to distract the dogs away from their baby ducklings which were hidden in amongst the dark reeds.

Tom and Molly knew the baby ducklings were hiding and tried hard to find them. They knelt down ever so quietly at the edge of the water, carefully separating the reeds ever so carefully. But those little ducklings did not like the intruders and swam swiftly, hiding themselves deeper into the thick of the reeds so Tom and Molly could not reach them.

"Ah Molly, look, there's a frog on the rock, "Tom stated, with a grin. He reached over, quickly grabbed it. Then stood up all excited to show Molly but just as he opened his hands the frog croaked then then jumped back into the water.

"Did you see him molly,' asked tom eagerly.

"Yes I did, 'Molly replied, with a big smile.

"Shame he got away from you Tom.'

"Yes, I would have loved to have kept him for a while, of well, maybe next time.'

Tom and Molly said good byes to the ducks and baby ducklings also the big green frog as they started to stroll off.

CHAPTER
THREE

Further across the field Molly seen a large mass of wild yellow daisies in amongst all the Patterson curse and long grass. The children ran over as fast as they could with Squiddle and Snookums at their sides.

"Lets pick some daisies, Tom'.

"Im starting over her Molly.'

Molly and Tom both decided to crouch down on their knees under the shade of a big old gum tree, while Squiddle also Snookums chased butterflies nearby.

The children made lots of neck laces plus bracelets with their daisy chains then they frolicked with Squiddle and Snookums having heaps of fun until Molly lay herself down on the soft green grass, in the shade, under a big gum tree.

Tom came over, he sat down beside her. Snookums and Squiddle settled quietly for a while next to Tom. Molly looked up, and was simply fascinated by the leaves that were

Shimmering from the sun.

"Look! ' Whispered Molly. "There's a nest of baby birds up there, Tom.'

Tom was mesmerized as, he laid down and watched the leaves not to mention the birds, for some time.

"Why do they keep chirping like that Tom?'

"Well they're hungry Molly, and they are waiting on their mother to return, to feed them."

A little later, Tom suggested that they better keep looking for Fluffy. Molly slowly stood up, and agreed then announced.

"I want to pick a bunch of daisies first before we go Tom, to take with me to give to mother."

"Don't take too long Molly." Tom replied, stretching his arms out to give Squiddle and Snoockums a pat then rubbing their tummies.

"I'm ready to go now." Molly eagerly said, with a smile.

As they continued through the field, birds were singing, bees were buzzing and pretty butterflies were fluttering. It was a glorious day.

CHAPTER FOUR

A short time later, they came across some sheep. A baby lamb stood still as Tom and Molly walked over swiftly then as they got closer walking slower, so they would not frighten the little lamb away. As Tom reached the little, he gave the lamb a pat as Molly put her arms around the little lamb's neck, giving it a hug. The little lamb bared...happily wagging its long tail ever so fast.

"Oh, he's so lovely,' Molly said to Tom.

"Yes,' Tom replied thoughtfully, feeling all warm inside.

Within the next few moments, Squiddle and Snookums came closer, they sniffed all over the little lamb busy checking it out. Tom and Molly giggled delightfully.

"Well Molly, I think we should keep going if we are going to try and looking for Fluffy.

"Bar..., bar...,' went the mother ewe, proudly calling out to her baby lamb. Molly let go of the lamb and watched, as it ran straight to its mother, than the little lamb latched onto its mother's teet to have a drink of milk.

CHAPTER FIVE

So, Tom and Molly started walking down the small hill until Tom seen some horses in the distance.

"Ah Molly, can you see those magnificent horses way over there?'

"No, where Tom,' his sister inquired.

"Just over there, near the old apple tree.' Tom replied eagerly, as he stretched out his arm and hand, showing Molly in which direction.

"Oh yes, I see them Tom. Can we go and pat them, please, please Tom.'

"Yes Molly, I want to go over and see them too!'

The children hurried along with Snookum and Squiddle by their sides, Tom quickly jumped over a pile of rocks meanwhile, Molly, Squiddle, Snookums decided to run around them.

"Here, hold, my hand Molly.' Tom sang out. Molly did, as she got close to him and they both ran all the way across the field. The horses were in a paddock fenced with high wire netting and joined to large wooden straining post.

Tom and Molly climbed up up on top of the wooden straining post all excited.

"Here horsie,' come on horsie,' said Tom, making a clicking noise with his mouth as he putting his hand out.

"Oh Tom, what's the matter with them. Why won't they come over to us?' Molly stated impatiently.

"They will, you just have to keep calling them Molly.'

Tom was feeling very confidant so he kept saying, " here horsies, here horse.'

When suddenly, the tall grey horse looked up, then started to stroll over to him. Molly didn't say anything, she just watch on, quite amazed.

"Oh Molly, what a splendid horse! ' Tom exclaimed, as the grey horse came over to the fence and Tom began to stroke it carefully.

Then Molly reached over, stretching her hand out a little reluctantly.

"Don't be afraid horsy,' Molly said nervously. " I won't hurt you.'

The grey mare just stood there, at the inside of the fence, which she seemed to be enjoying the attention, as Tom and Molly continued to pat her. Molly's eyes were gleaming and wide open with excitement, then it wasn't long before the other three horses wondered over with their heads down, swishing their tails pleased to have Molly, as well as Tom pat them.

"There are rather friendly, 'said Molly.

"I wonder if they would like some grass to eat? 'Tom inquired.

"Yes, I think so Tom.'

So Tom climbed down off the fence then started to pick a huge handful of grass.

"Here you are Molly, you take this handful and I'll pick some more some more for me.'

"Thank you.' Molly replied nicely with a pleasing smile on her face.

But, as Tom knelt down, he was even more, so surprised. 'It's a lizard.' He sang out loudly.

Tom gently got hold of him, he was ever so careful not to hurt the lizard in any way.

"Look Molly,' said Tom, as he slowly climbed back up apon the post strainer next to Molly, and put his hands up close to her, Molly screamed, she dropped her handful of grass and she quickly jumped down off the fence and kept a bit of a distance from Tom. Molly was horrified, as she didn't like lizards of any kind.

"Don't be scared, Molly, lizards will not hurt you.' Tom replied, to her caringly, but also tormenting slightly.

"Still, Molly was not convinced,' as she stated, quite flustered.

"You know I don't like lizards, Tom!'

"Well, I let him go then.'

"I should think so.' Molly stated, being a bit of a bossy boots, shying a little further from Tom.

"But, make sure you let him go way over there, near that tree.'

"Tom laughed and laughed.' As he ran toward Molly, scaring her even more so, Molly screamed so loud, she near defended Tom, but she finally stopped as Tom started walking toward the tree nearby.

Tom reached the tree, and said, softly to himself, "There you go little lizard, I will place you here in amongst the soft green grass under the shade but near the trunk of the tree for protection.'

CHAPTER
SIX

The afternoon sun shone as a gentle breeze blew. Tom, Molly, Squiddle and Snookum's ventured furthure across the field wandering were Fluffy might be.

They came upon a stream, filled with fresh running rippled water. Squiddle and Snookums were so pleased, as they were very thirsty. They raced over to have a drink.

Molly and Tom joined them. The grass was soft, as they laid themselves down on their tummies at the very edge, placing their arms out then cuffing their hands together, sipping the water out of their hands.

"Ah..., I was thirsty,' said Tom.

"So was I,' Molly replied.

After Tom had finished having a drink of the cool refreshing water, he glanced at Squiddle, then Snookums, then laughed.

"Look Molly, there's a blackberry bush.'

"Hoorah', said Molly. As she stood up ever so anxiously.

"I'm hungry Tom, let's pick some?'

"Oh yes, Molly, I'm hungry too!'

Tom and Molly helped themselves, until they were so full of the blackberries that they couldn't eat another one. They had blackberry juice all over their faces and strains on their hands. Happy, Tom and Molly sat down next to a weeping willow tree. It was one of many that lined the edge of a beautiful, stream that was a back drop from the river.

Tom and Molly laid back, just letting the soft green grass merely cushion their bodies, as they took in splendor. Meanwhile, they listening to the water running, wild ducks quacking on the other side of the river, frogs croaking, birds chirping, horse flies, white moths and butterflies fluttering. Birds singing, bee's buzzing, dogs barking, as the spring sun shone down on them, with a gentle breeze blew just leaving a heavenly scent of perfume, from the wild daisies and the pretty Patterson curse that was in the distance, as they laid down again for a while, they watched the blue gums leaves changing colour as the breeze was heavenly, also the willow that were gracefully swaying, just touching, the top of the water of the river.

Molly couldn't help thinking, about how lucky she was, to live in the country.

CHAPTER SEVEN

"Molly, look over there.'

Molly looked in the direction that Tom was pointing too, and seen nothing

"Look again Molly,' said Tom. " There's a big red buck kangaroo, way over there near those trees.'

Molly kept searching straight ahead, and before too long.

"Yes, I can see the kangaroo now,' Molly remarked anxiously.

"And there's another one, Molly, can you see it.'

"Oh yes,' stated Molly.

"But Molly, looked at what jumped out next to them.'

"Oh Tom, it's a baby kangaroo.'

"Yes Molly.'

"Yes Molly, it's called a joey.'

"Is it,' laughed Molly.

The children watched the kangaroo's feeding on the grass for a short time in total delight.

"The kangaroo's will come down for a drink at sundown Molly, but I suppose if they are really thirsty they might all venture down where we were at, in the back drop water.

"It is a great place, which looks like a lovely place to paddle. But mother as well as father, always told us never get to close to the river.'

Molly was a little concerned as she asked, "Tom, the kangaroo's won't go past us, as we are half way near them and the water.'

"No Molly, they are just as worried about us as we are of them, well that's what dad told me.' Molly sighed with relief.'

The children were delightfully curious as they watched the kangaroo's at a distance. There were grey ones and a lot of red one's too. But the little baby joey's were quite adorable, as Tom and Molly watched them, hopping around not to fare from their mother's. Meanwhile, some tinnier joey's were quite contented to stay in their mother's pouches, with their little heads sticking out.

CHAPTER EIGHT

Tom suddenly became distracted. and said, " Come on Molly, it's about this time of day that fish start feeding on the top of the water.'

They were not too far from where that beautiful spot was with the back flow from the river, that left a nice and safe place to have paddle or swim, but it wasn't quite hot enough for Tom or Molly to do so. But as Tom and Molly ventured down the hill then on the flat pasture until they were finally there, they were very excited even Squiddle and Snookums they started to bark chasing each other than playfully had a scuff, ruffing one another up until it became a bit serious and Tom had to put a stop to them by rousing on them, the they settled down.

"Look Molly, did you see that fish come to the top of the water.'

"Tom, they're playing.' Molly said, with extreme excitement as she laid herself down in the soft green grass, on her tummy near the edge of the water.

"No, Molly, the fish are feeding on top of the water.

"Why Tom? Molly asked.

"Well Molly, there are a lot of tiny insects on the surface of the water having a drink, so the fish feed of them.'

"So Tom, what sort of insects do they eat?' Molly asked? In total amazement." They eat dragonflies, bugs, white moths, flies and all

Sorts of tiny insects.'

"Molly asked Tom, why they eat all those very pretty insects.' Molly whispered to herself, they are so beautiful.'

Tom stood up then dusted himself down, and stated, "come on Molly it's time to go.'

So Molly said her goodbyes, as she looked back, to what looked like a beautiful fairy land, that she would dream about tonight, then ran to catch up to Tom.

CHAPTER NINE

The children wondered across the meadow until they came to a dirt pathway in the middle of lots of tree's which took them further on, near some bushes.

"Tom, do you think Fluffy would be in here somewhere?'

"Fluffy cold be anywhere Molly, you just have to keep looking!' Tom stated, as he searched through a lot of tall shrubs.

"Molly she seen some Emu's that were heading straight towards her. She screamed,' Tom ran to her so quickly.

"What's wrong?' he asked quickly.

Molly pointed to the Emu's, swiftly Tom grabbed Molly's hand and they both ran as fast as they could. Squiddle and Snookums seen all the Emu's, they ran so fast that they beat Tom and Molly.

Before long, Squiddle, Snookums and the children came out of the trees than ran up on the hill. They stopped, so did the dogs, while they caught their breath, Tom and Molly looked to see to see if the Emu's were still chasing them, but the Emu's headed down towards the stream, for a drink.

Tom and Molly watched when they ran past them when they ran past. The Emu's were covered with large black and gray feathers plus, they had big black eye's which, was enough to let Tom and Molly know not to get to close to them.

With a big sigh, the children hurried along, and continued on their merry way, looking for Fluffy.

Not too far along they came across some logs just under the branches of a beautiful peppercorn tree. The children stopped, and searched in all the logs and beneath long branches. But, Molly's little Fluffy, Her rabbit was nowhere to be seen.

"Where could my Fluffy be?' Molly asked, Tom.

"I don't know.' Tom said sympathetically.

"But, we will find him, Molly.'

"What will happen Tom, if we cannot find him?'

"Fluffy is not lost Molly, he has just hidden himself somewhere.'

"Oh dear.' Cried Molly.

"I do hope we find him soon.'

CHAPTER
TEN

A little later, when the children walk slowly and reached the other paddock, they climbed up on wire netting fence then looked out. All of sudden, Tom and Molly heard this fearful noise. It was a big ferocious bull.

Instantly, Squiddle Snookums bristles went up, on their backs. Meanwhile, the loud barking as the bull started to tear up the ground, was deafening, as Tom, Molly were definitely fearful Molly and Tom quickly jumped down off the fence, running away with Squiddle and Suookums down the hill until?

They came to an old gum tree. The children stopped to catch their breath, while Sqiddle as well as Snookums laid down on the grass, puffing and panting. Patting Poor Snookums also Squiddle, they were ever so pleased to be away from that big black bull too. Now they were all safe.

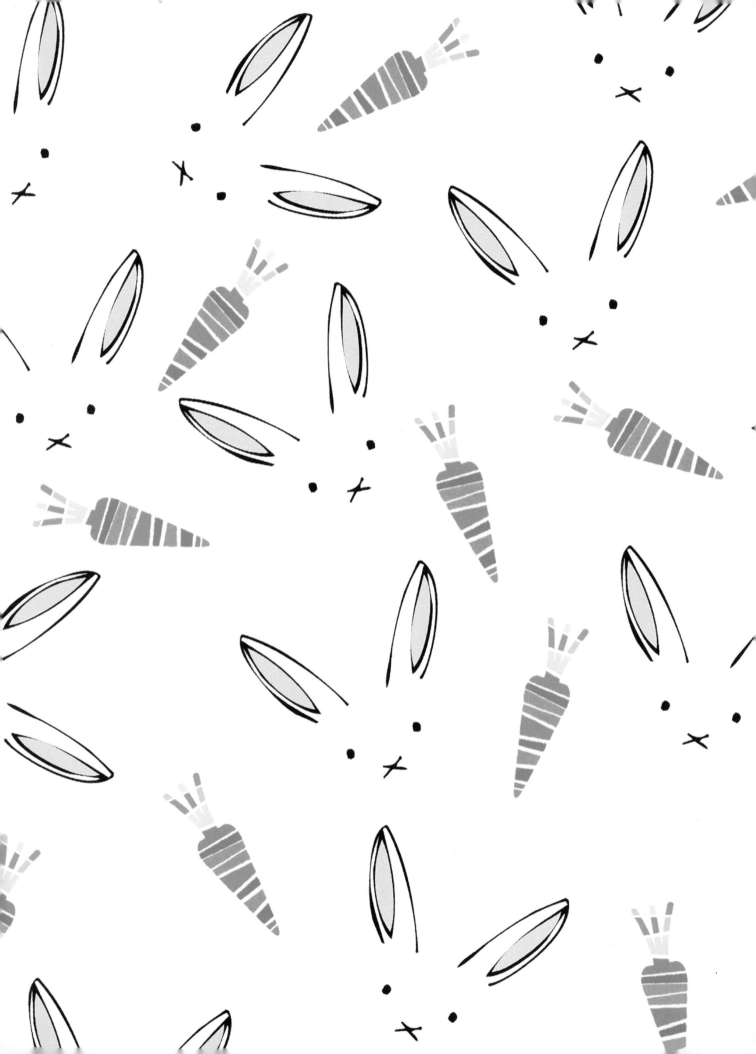

CHAPTER ELEVEN

Squiddle also Snookums started to pounce for joy, jumping up on Molly and Tom which they both eagerly gave them pats which, turned out to be tummy rubs.

"Molly I think you better pick some fresh daisies and Patterson cure for mother, those one look terrible.

"Come for a walk just over there, and I pay with the dogs while you get some more.'

Molly got a nice bunch of flowers for mum, she placed them gently down on the grass.

"I'm going to play roly-polys, down the hill, Tom do you want to play too.'

"Yes, Molly hang on and I will take my back pack off, then we will go, and see who gets down the bottom first.'

"Yes, that's good, Molly gave Tom a couple of minutes, and we will go on the count off three.'

So off they went, laughing their heads off, but Tom got down to the bottom first.

Tom and molly got up and dusted.

." I'm still got a lot of grass on me, so have you Tom.'

"It doesn't matter, we had fun.'

Then he picked up his bag while Molly gently picked up her flowers for her mother.

"Look,' Tom said, clowning around with Molly, then he slowly stopped.

"Molly, I'm not sure but over there in the distance, if it's a stack of wood or some fox burrows.'

"Do you want to go and see?'

"Alright then.'

Molly, Tom, Squiddle and Snookums strutted across the field then down a bit. A large flock of cockatoo's flew over above them, making a lot of noise, and squeaking and squawking until, they settled down on the branches in the trees nearby. As the Tom and Molly got closer, Tom stopped, the put his arm out so, Molly wouldn't go any further also.

"What's wrong?' Molly asked.

"Shoosh,' Tom whispered.

"Why?' Molly whispered.

"Because Molly, that pile of wood in front of us, well, is not just woods and sticks there Molly. It looks like to me that there are a couple of rabbit burrows, as well.'

"Do think Tom, that Fluffy could be in one of the burrows. Molly whispered.'

"Yes Molly, now be very quiet otherwise if Fluffy is in one of the burrows, he won't know it's us and we will frighten him away, then we might not be able to catch him.'

As Tom and Molly slowly also quietly reach the burrows stated to get excited.

"Tom whispered to Molly, go to the end of that burrow and get ready to catch Fluffy if he comes running out, no you quietly take this strong stick wait until I get to the other end of the burrow, when I give you the signal with my hand you put the stick inside your end, then go round and around meanwhile, I will get ready to catch Fluffy, that's if Fluffy's in there, now wait until I'm ready then I will give you the signal, with my hand waving at you.'

Tom crouched down, when he was ready he gave Molly the signal. Molly twirled and poke her stick so hopefully, if Fluffy was in there he would come out Tom's end but, at the same time she was ready to grab Fluffy if he came out her end of the burrow.

A few moments went by when Fluffy came out of the burrow and ran into Tom's arms.

"I've got him Molly,' Tom said, with total delight.

"It's Fluffy, it's Fluffy, yeah,' Molly could help herself, she was over the moon with pure pleasure and total delight as she ran around to Tom. Molly petted him ever so lovingly.

"Can I hold him Tom, please, please?'

"No Molly you better not, he might jump out of your arms, how about I put him in my back pack which I will carry in front of me, so he doesn't get away also Fluffy will feel safe until we get home.'

"Well Molly, I think we better start heading for home.'

"Yes Tom, but I'm so happy that we found Fluffy, aren't you?'

"Of course I am, I'm just as happy as you.'

The children began walking across the meadow then down the hill a bit, until they came to the main road that would take them to their home.

"Tom isn't just wonderful that we found Fluffy, I'm so excited and relieved at the same time.'

"Yes Molly, I'm so happy too."

Tom kept a soft but firm hold on Fluffy so he wouldn't get away on him, meanwhile, Molly kept cutting across in front of Tom almost tripping him over, as she attempted to keep patting Fluffy's little head that was sticking out of one of the side gaps.

"Molly, please try and stop stepping in front of me, otherwise I might trip then fall.'

"I'm so sorry Tom, I won't do it again.'

"Tom, do you remember that you said, that mother gave you a couple of drinks to take with us?'

"Yes Molly, I do.'

Tom stopped walking after a while then bent down, Snookums was all over him, she wanted some love and attention.'

Meanwhile, Molly and Squiddle also stopped, while they waited for Tom as he had to be careful not to let Fluffy out while he got the drinks.

"Now Molly, the drink that mother gave me was very warm when we were at the back flow of the river so, I tipped them out, but I filled them up with fresh water like father had taught me when we went fishing.'

"After Tom had a drink, he tried to give Fluffy a drink out of his hand, poor Fluffy didn't get much.

Molly quickly had a drink out of her bottle then spotted some wild flowers.

"Wait a minute Tom, while I quickly pick mother a fresh bunch of flowers as the last bunch doesn't look to good.'

"Alright Molly," so Tom sat down patiently and played with Squiddle, fluffy hid back into the bag,

Tom sang out," are you ready yet?"

"Yes, I'm happy now.'

The children walked along with all their pets, and headed back towards the main road that took them home. The children may have walked long and wide, they were both getting tired, but it took them awhile but they were nearly home.

"Molly, you must be getting tired by now.' Tom inquired.

And just as Molly was going to reply to Tom a flock of wild ducks flew over the top of Tom and Molly's heads which they landed nearby, in front of their main home paddock, where there was a small natural spring there all the time, their feathers were different colours and their beak's too, were different from normal ducks. The ducks landed, on the spring that they have been doing every year.

"Well Molly, were home, and with Fluffy.

"Yes Tom, my day was wonderful, I don't think I will ever forget it, also, thank you so much for finding Fluff for me.'

Molly gave Tom a big cuddle and thought of all the wonderful animals that they had seen most of all, she enjoyed when they stayed at the back flow of the river, having mulberries, laying in the soft green grass with all the beautiful butterflies white moths, with all their wonderful different colours, which were like fairies, that was just like one of her favorite fairy books she had at home.

Dedication

I would dearly like to thank my son Jason, my daughter Angelina, and my loving youngest daughter Michelle, my grandson Sam, and my lovely grand daughter Sarah, which once again I was lucky enough to have that loving inspiration which has left me with the true Wonders of the Wonders of life.s

Julie Abnett

CPSIA information can be obtained
at www.ICGtesting.com
Printed in the USA
BVHW021613060819
555209BV00004B/10/P